A BREATHTAKING TALE OF DISCOVERY

FALL IN
LOVE AGAIN

LILY ANAND

NewDelhi • London

BLUEROSE PUBLISHERS
India | U.K.

Copyright © Lily Anand 2023

All rights reserved by author. No part of this publication may be reproduced, stored in a retrieval system or transmitted in any form or by any means, electronic, mechanical, photocopying, recording or otherwise, without the prior permission of the author. Although every precaution has been taken to verify the accuracy of the information contained herein, the publisher assumes no responsibility for any errors or omissions. No liability is assumed for damages that may result from the use of information contained within.

BlueRose Publishers takes no responsibility for any damages, losses, or liabilities that may arise from the use or misuse of the information, products, or services provided in this publication.

For permissions requests or inquiries regarding this publication, please contact:

BLUEROSE PUBLISHERS
www.BlueRoseONE.com
info@bluerosepublishers.com
+91 8882 898 898
+4407342408967

ISBN: 978-93-5819-257-5

Cover design: Muskan Sachdeva
Typesetting: Rohit

First Edition: December 2023

Introduction

Hello everyone! I'm excited to welcome you to the world of "Royal Love," the first book in the Royal Series. Before you start reading, I want to let you know that this is a work of fiction, which means that everything you'll read is purely from my imagination. I hope you'll enjoy exploring this fictional universe and let your imagination run wild.

My name is Sukhawant Kaur Anand, but I write under the pen name Lily Anand. "Royal Love" is my first book, and I'm both excited and humbled to share it with you. I hope the story will transport you to a world filled with romance, intrigue, and royalty.

As you read through the book, I encourage you to get lost in the characters' lives and the vivid landscapes described in the story. I believe that storytelling has the power to captivate and transport readers, and I hope "Royal Love" will do just that for you.

At the heart of this story is a belief that every woman has hidden power within her waiting to be unleashed. I hope the characters and events in the book will inspire you to embrace your strength, resilience, and unique essence.

So, please enjoy reading "Royal Love." Let the words take you on a journey, and may the characters stay with you long after you finish reading. Thank you for joining me on this adventure, and I hope you'll find as much joy in reading as I did in writing this book.

Happy reading!

Character Profiles:

Sheikh Ajmal Bin Shalik - A formidable business tycoon, scion of the royal family, yet devoid of greed, arrogance, and selfishness.

Molly Cohan - A spirited photographer, self-made and devoted to her daughter Noor.

John Cohan - Molly's doting father, endlessly supportive of Molly and Noor.

Noor - The vivacious, charming daughter of Ajmal and Molly, a bundle of joy.

Contents

The chance meeting. 1

Whispers of Love. 4

Your Highness. 7

Noor. 10

Revelations. 14

A Royal Proposal. 18

Love in the air. 24

Mix Up Feelings 28

Preprations. 40

Accident. 50

The Grand Wedding. 54

Early Days Of Royalty. 60

The Mysterious Letter. 70

Author's Note 74

Chapter 1

The chance meeting.

Ajmal and Molly's Journey: "He was my first love, the keeper of my heart. Then he became my heartbreaker, vanishing from my life. What went wrong, and why did he return? How is my fate intertwined with his? Ten years have passed, and I shouldn't let him see my weakness. I clutched my fist, enduring the pain, knowing he had inflicted deeper wounds. I mustn't look into his eyes, for he has the power to consume me once more. He's not the same person - his appearance, attitude, everything has transformed."

"Molly Cohan, a beautiful woman who cherishes happiness but has tasted the pain of love. Is Ajmal plotting to break her heart again after a decade apart? Can they find true love again, perhaps with someone very special to her? Join us on their journey of love. What occurs when their eyes meet... sparks fly, and hearts get scorched. A single night of passion was all it took for Ajmal to walk away from Molly."

Molly Cohan's Perspective: "Sheikh Ajmal Bin Shalik," Molly stared in disbelief at the familiar face on the glossy magazine cover. Ten years had passed, but it felt like yesterday. Today, she would meet him again, yearning to scratch his face with her painted nails, to inflict upon him the same pain he had once inflicted upon her - a pain that left her broken both physically and emotionally.

"Are you okay?" Ric asked, concerned. Molly glanced at Ajmal's picture and replied, "Sure," though her focus remained on him. "Tell me more about him."

Ric sighed, "I knew you weren't listening. This is Sheikh Ajmal Bin Shalik. He's meeting the president at ten. It's your typical goodwill event between nations, but the boss wants pictures. Any country willing to give the U.S. first access to its oil reserves is good for a press release. You better capture some great shots, dear; I'll handle the interviews."

Molly nodded and probed, "What do you know about him?" Ric hesitated, "I don't know much, but he's royalty, quite the ladies' man, a notorious playboy. He was once married to an actress and a French model, but they are no longer with us. He's a billionaire with numerous business ventures and two younger married brothers. Well, you're quite the one to speak with, Molly," she commented, taking in the news.

Molly remained professional, prepared with her cameras, lenses, and a dozen rolls of film. The weight was familiar, comforting, and empowering. Passing the security guards with a friendly smile, she entered the hall where the meeting would take place, wondering how she would react when she saw him.

Sheikh Ajmal Bin Shalik, accompanied by the ambassador and the president, graced the stage adorned with fragrant flowers. The hall was filled with the sweet scent of blossoms. As she approached the cluster of microphones, dignitaries and staff from both nations stood on one side, and professionals like her stood on the other.

Ajmal's visit to the US held a special significance. One reason was the impending treaty to be signed, while the other was a quest for his lost love, Molly, who had remained in his heart as his heartbeat and the love of his life for the past ten years. The distance to the barrage of microphones was short, with dignitaries and staff members from both nations following suit. Tight security was in place. Ajmal planned to take a few days of vacation and then embark on a search for Molly, who had mysteriously disappeared a decade ago. Despite his earlier attempts to locate her, she seemed to have vanished into thin air, and now, he was determined to find her.

Adjusting his formal kaftan, Ajmal stood beside the president with his ministers, all adorned in Arab attire, a source of pride for him. Memories flooded back as he pondered her whereabouts and what might have happened to her. President's address to the crowd began, and Ajmal's gaze locked onto a young woman positioned behind a camera. For a moment, he thought he recognized her, and as she focused on him, shock crossed his face. He could see her fingers snapping and trembling before she dropped her camera. Their eyes met, and she coolly changed the lens, revealing herself to be Molly.

Shocked, Ajmal stared at her, realizing that fate had brought them together again. He planned to send someone to call her; she had a lot of explaining to do about the past ten years. In his eyes, she was his and only his – the present love of Sheikh Ajmal Bin Shalik.

Chapter 2

Whispers of Love.

Molly was equally shocked by Ajmal's sudden appearance, sensing the myriad of questions in his eyes. Despite the astonishment, Ajmal composed himself and delivered his speech in flawless English. However, his heart churned as he glanced toward Molly. After expressing gratitude to the president, he turned to find her, but she had disappeared once again.

Choosing not to answer Ric's questions, Molly swiftly left the crowd after the ceremony, opting for the company's van to return to the office to finish her pending tasks. The desire to burn the pictures of Ajmal surged within her. Despite their apparent love, he had concealed his true identity, appearing as a charming, lovable college kid with shared hobbies. Now knowing him as Arabian Royalty, Molly vowed never to fall for him again.

She questioned herself for having been so crazy in love with him, sharing her body, discussing marriage, unaware of his royal status. The thought of the past gave her a splitting headache, and Ric found her in the office, head bowed on the table.

"Ric... where did you disappear, and why did you drive back alone?" he suddenly asked her.

"Stop it, Ric. I already have a splitting headache," I told him.

Ric began reading Ajmal's profile, saying, "Wow, Molly, this Sheikh Ajmal has done schooling in England. Although he is a ladies' man, always flirting with models and actresses, he married Susan, the French model-come-actress. Oh, she died a few years back."

"Just stop, Ric," I said.

"Hey, sweetheart, what's up?" Ric asked. "Why so agitated today?"

"Nothing, Ric. Dead tired," I replied.

Ric continued reading, "No kids, he is closer to his two younger brothers; they were married." He closed the file and left, saying, "He is in his cabin; you can call him if needed."

"I kept thinking about how the past struggles had changed me from a sweet, bubbly girl to a mature, responsible single mother. I went through a tough pregnancy, survived doing different petty jobs, left college due to pregnancy, and turned my hobby of photography into a profession. With luck and hard work, I am now working at Sentinel, a famous firm—all with the help of my best friend," I thought. I snapped back to the present, picked up my car keys, and left for home. Noor must be waiting, and I had to cook her favorite pasta.

As I reached home, I received a message that Noor was with her friend, which relieved me. I didn't want her to see me in this state of anxiety. The next morning, my phone rang, and it was Dad. A smile came to my face as I answered, "How are you, princess?" he asked. "I'm good," I replied. I never told him my sorrows and pain, especially about Ajmal. He asked, "So, princess, when are you coming to meet me?" "I will think about it," I said. "Please, baby, come. I want to meet you both soon," he insisted. "Yeah, Papa, I will make plans soon," I replied, smiling, and hung up.

Oh my god, it was Saturday, and I had a lot to do—mow the garden, wash the car, cook, clean, and do laundry. As Noor had not returned from her friend's place, I started mowing the garden. When I was about to finish, I saw a car stop, and a man climbed out from the front to open the back door. I thought of running but couldn't move. Oh my god, Sheikh Ajmal Bin Shalik climbed out and surveyed my house from behind his dark glasses. I was almost trembling; he looked so hot and dashing. He was tall, very good looking, and now I knew where Noor got her looks. She was an exact copy of her father, except she took my color—fair with pink cheeks, long hair, tall for her age, and extra brainy.

Ajmal's eyes scanned me as he walked towards me. I must be twenty-eight or nine now, but he smiled warmly, making me feel young and beautiful as ever, even in my morning track pants. I gave him a grumpy look when he said, "Hi dear" and then "Hi, Molly" with his sweetest smile. I just nodded my head. "Well, should I bow to you, Your Highness, or whatever courtesy calls are in your nation?" I remarked. "Neither. A simple 'Hello' will do," he replied. I gave him a long stare without a smile and said, "I don't have servants, Your Highness, so I can't offer you any drinks. Just say what you have to say, then please leave, as I'm very busy today."

Chapter 3

Your Highness.

He kept looking at me and smiled patiently. "I will just have water, and can you just take me inside? It's so hot outside. It took me all yesterday to locate you, and you are throwing a tantrum. I was very angry with you, just leaving without acknowledging me. Why? You tell me. Why should I take you inside? You are a stranger, from nowhere, and I don't entertain any Tom, Dick inside my house." Sheikh came closer, reached out to brush my curl from my face, and said, "Please, dear, let's talk inside." He caught hold of my hand, went towards the main door, and said, "Now you can call me Sheikh or Ajmal or honey, whichever you prefer," looking into my eyes.

The touch of his fingers brought forth memories from the past, and she flushed with warmth. Taking a breath, she caught the scent of his aftershave, momentarily leaving her breathless.

Molly ushered him inside, and as he surveyed her living room, he seemed surprised by the well-done interior, adorned in pastel shades of greens, creams, and a hint of pink here and there. Indoor plants and flower pots added to the charm.

Ajmal's eyes returned to her, and in a soft voice filled with warmth, he asked, "How have you been, honey?" He expressed a desire to explain why he left suddenly ten years ago, tears welling up in her eyes. Molly questioned why he even tried to reach her after disappearing, especially after promising marriage. Tears flowed uncontrollably, as if a flood of the past ten years had surged back. She turned away, attempting to conceal her grief, but he was by her side in an instant, holding her close as she cried into his chest. It felt like coming home, as if they were back in each other's arms after an eternity.

At that very moment, Noor entered, asking, "Hi mom, and who is he, whom you are hugging so sweetly? Your friend?" Molly released herself from Ajmal's arms and hugged her daughter. "Yes, baby, an old friend meeting after a very long time. Say hi to him." Ajmal, shocked within, managed a smile and greeted Noor, suggesting a ride in his limo, which excited her.

Upon their return, Molly sent Noor to her room for cleanup. Standing in the doorway, Sheikh asked, "How old is your daughter?" with a stern expression. Molly requested clarification, and he pressed further, accusing her of playing games and demanding to know when she was going to reveal the truth.

Molly, taken aback, looked away, surprised that he hadn't recognized Noor, his own blood. She took a deep breath and replied, "Actually, I don't believe this is any of your business."

Before more words could escape her lips, he crossed the room in two strides and grabbed her arms. Molly demanded to be let go, expressing her disbelief at his audacity after hiding his true identity and leaving without a proper goodbye.

"Allah, give me strength," he muttered. Molly insisted, "Let me go, Aj. How dare you come after so many years and put allegations on me? Who gave you the right to ask me all this when you hid your true identity and left without saying goodbye?"

"Allah," Ajmal sighed, "It wasn't lies, but I couldn't tell you due to security reasons. I was waiting for the right time to reveal my love. I swear, dear, on Allah, I'm not lying."

Emotions filled his eyes, tears streaming down his face. "I swear."

She shook her head, and he came closer to her. His hands were warm and hard, and despite his grip, she felt tingles in her body. Their foreheads met, and his warm breath sent confusing signals to her body. He gave her a peck on her lips and said, "Let's meet tomorrow, please Doll." His thumb traced the outline of her lips, then moved to the line of her collarbone. She couldn't think straight with butterflies in her stomach. Trying to untangle from his arms, she realized his grip was tight.

She attempted to free herself, saying, "Not here, Ajj..." He responded, "Okay, tomorrow, we'll meet at my hotel. I'll send the car."

"I don't know," she shook her head. He smiled and confidently said, "I do." With his fingertip, he touched her cheek and tipped her chin up, gazing into her light brown eyes. "I'll send the car at one, then we will talk." Slowly, he lowered his face until his lips brushed hers. He reluctantly let her go when Noor's voice came from her room, and he left without looking back.

Chapter 4

Noor.

Staring at him, Molly listened to his quick strides down the hall, to the front door opening and closing. Noor entered, excited about the limo, expressing her desire to be a princess and wave from the window.

Molly was struck by the thought that Noor might have been a princess if they were still together. Doubts about her decision not to tell Ajmal about his daughter crept in. She informed Noor about her lunch meeting the next day, and Noor reassured her, mentioning her friend Sephie's visit.

The next day, Molly headed to Ajmal's hotel. The weather was cool and beautiful, and the chauffeur stopped at the hotel's portico. An Arab escort guided her to the elevator, and within moments, they were in a very elegant room. Ajmal, wearing a blue polo shirt and cream-colored slacks, stood up, looking handsome. Molly had conflicting thoughts but reminded herself to convey that it would be their last meeting.

He rose to meet her eyes, causing shivers, and she stayed near the lift that had brought her straight to his room. Molly immediately confronted him about leaving her alone ten years ago. Ajmal explained that his father had suffered a major heart attack on the day he left Molly, and he was commanded to return. He clarified that his father used the excuse to call him back, and he had to follow his wishes as the heir to the royalty.

Ajmal shared that Molly's place was checked regularly, and he had sent letters and cablegrams, but they all came back. Molly questioned why he didn't inform her about his situation, and he explained the controlling nature of the circumstances. Molly decided to leave, but Ajmal insisted there was more to discuss.

As Molly headed towards the lift, Ajmal commanded her to stay, and she responded, "Maybe in your country you can order people, but I don't take orders from anyone." Ajmal urged her to sit, claiming they had a lot to catch up on, and Molly hesitated but eventually turned back.

Ajmal expressed that there was still love between them and wanted to know about her life. Molly, still cautious, shared a bit about herself. Ajmal continued to press her for details, revealing that she had always been in his heart. He inquired about her marital status and her father's well-being. The conversation unfolded, emotions resurfacing as they navigated the complexities of the past.

Molly responded, "Oh my myyyy, like you were married with me in your heart, stop lying Aj," she said. "My marriage was an arrangement, dear. When I got the impression you had stopped responding, I could not locate you, so then I gave in, and then my father forced me into this."

"Don't throw this marriage fiasco into my face when you wasted no time to replace me with someone else," Ajmal retorted. "Did you love him? Noor's father."

She shrugged and said, "I thought I did, as much as you loved me."

"No, dear," Ajmal said, "was I a passing fling in college? Did I mean nothing to you? You found your lover very soon after I left."

"Never mind, the past is over. I need to go home," Molly stated.

"Tell me, how old is Noor and in which grade is she studying? Does she have a passport or not?"

"Why are you asking? Because when I return, I want you with me."

"That's not possible. I came to tell you let's move on and forget about the past. By the way, Ajmal, were you engaged with your wife?" she asked abruptly.

"Since childhood," he answered.

"I don't believe this, Ajmal. All the time you were having an affair with me, you were engaged to someone. All the time we were together, you were someone else's. You didn't have any shame using me, my heart, my emotions, even my body."

"No, you are changing the situation. It was never me. There was nothing between myself and Sasela until you married Ajmal----Sheikh. Now you can't throw stones at me. Even you took a lover very soon, Molly," Ajmal lashed out.

Molly clamped her lips tight; she was all red with anger. She glared at him and said, "Now can I leave, your Highness?"

"Stay for dinner."

"No."

"Stay for dinner. Let's start fresh. I can send for your daughter. She can eat with us."

"No?"

Ajmal questioned, "Why is she avoiding me meeting her daughter? Am I missing something? Is she hiding something?" He watched her, realizing she wasn't indifferent to him.

"What is she hiding?" he thought. "Foolish girl, I will find out, and I will never let you go. Now I have found you."

Suddenly, he asked, "Heyy, why did you cut your long hair?" He grabbed her suddenly in his arms, "You knew I loved your long silky hair. How many men have you let play with your hair? Tell me? Whom all have you had an affair with?" His hands reached her shoulder as his gaze held hers.

"How mannnnnyyy," he demanded. She wanted to lie, but she could not.

"None," she whispered, feeling his fingers tightening at her shoulder. He kissed her on her forehead and released her. "I will call my assistant to escort you back home," he said, stepping back to where his phone was lying on the table.

Suddenly, she froze. God, she thought, let him not remember that night. Sheikh watched her leave from his room. It was time to establish his family again. He smiled at the very thought. He called his assistant, Salid.

"Is there anything you require, sir?" he asked me. "Yes, Salid, the woman who was just here has a daughter. Please find about her birth certificate, then send a big box of chocolates to her residence and a very big bouquet of flowers to her office."

Ajmal was not feeling good thinking about Noor's father. He wanted to know everything about her past years.

Molly reached home late, tired both mentally and physically. First, the worry of seeing him, then being confronted with him. Switching on lights, she headed for the phone to call Noor to come home. She was missing her Doll; she would call her friend next day.

When she reached the office in the morning, there was a big ruckus outside her cabin. Even before entering the office, she got greetings and smiles from guards and security people. She was very confused, as today was not her birthday. When the receptionist said,

Chapter 5

Revelations.

"Good morning, ma'am, what beautiful flowers. We never knew you had a secret admirer. You are lucky, ma'am." As she entered her cabin, she saw beautiful bunches of roses, lilies, carnations. They were placed in every corner of her room.

"Oh my God, he never forgot my love for daisies and lilies. They were so breathtaking. I was zapped for a second when I came inside the room." All her fellow colleagues, friends, journalists, and editors were packed in her room. They were all waiting for her to open the envelope on the main beautiful exotic flowers bunch, which was on the center of the table. She kept her cameras aside and reached for the envelope. Inside, it read, "Have dinner with me tonight. Yours only."

"Wow, everyone clapped, lovely admirer." A very close and rich friend remarked, "You know how to keep secrets." Putting up a smile in front of everyone, she smiled and distributed those bunches to all, except the center one.

Ric entered the office, saying, "Well, friends, all back to work. I need to have a word with Molly." After giving her a cup of coffee, he asked, "Care to tell me all about this, or secrets from me also, your friend and partner?"

Ajmal smiled and said, "You're taking a lot of time, my dear. I hope you're picking something that complements your beauty." His compliment made her blush, and she replied, "I just want to make sure I look nice, considering it's your friend's reception."

They eventually left for the reception in one of Ajmal's elegant cars. The event was grand, filled with opulence and grandeur. Molly, dressed in a stunning outfit, felt a bit overwhelmed by the extravagance, but she tried to enjoy the evening.

Throughout the reception, Ajmal introduced Molly to his friends and business associates. He was attentive and proud to have her by his side. She couldn't help but notice how well he fit into this world of wealth and power, and it made her realize how different their lives had become over the years.

As the night progressed, Molly found herself having a great time. The music was lively, the food was delicious, and Noor was excited about the whole experience. She danced with her daughter, and even Ajmal joined them on the dance floor. Molly couldn't deny that she was enjoying herself.

Later in the evening, when they were sitting at a quiet corner of the venue, Ajmal looked at Molly with a serious expression. "Molly, I want to talk to you about something," he began. She looked at him, unsure of what to expect.

"What is it, Ajmal?" she asked.

He took a deep breath and said, "I know that things have changed, and I understand that we both have separate lives now. But seeing you tonight, being with you and Noor, I can't help but feel that there's something special between us. Molly, I want to try and rebuild what we once had. I want to be a part of your and Noor's life, and I want us to be a family again."

Molly was taken aback by his words. She had tried so hard to move on and build a life for herself and Noor, and now Ajmal was asking for something she hadn't expected. She looked at him, her emotions swirling inside.

Before she could respond, Noor, who had been playing nearby, came over and hugged both of them. She looked up at Molly and Ajmal, her eyes filled with hope and happiness.

Molly couldn't deny that a part of her still cared for Ajmal, and the idea of Noor having her father back was heartwarming. But she also knew that it wasn't that simple. Their past had been filled with complications, and she needed time to think.

"Let's talk about this later, Ajmal," Molly said softly, "For now, let's enjoy this evening and make it a memorable one for Noor."

Ajmal nodded, understanding that Molly needed time to process his unexpected proposal. They continued to enjoy the rest of the evening, dancing, and creating beautiful memories as a family, albeit a complicated one.

Molly's head was spinning with conflicting emotions as Ajmal pressed her about Noor's paternity. She took a deep breath and replied firmly, "Ajmal, Noor is my daughter, and she is not anyone's possession. You left, and I had no choice but to face everything alone. Noor is the result of that loneliness, and she's mine. I never had the luxury of your support or the comfort of knowing you'd be there for us."

Ajmal's gaze bore into her, and she continued, "You have no right to demand information about her father. Noor is happy and loved, and that's what matters."

His eyes softened, and he sighed. "Molly, I never meant to hurt you, and I understand I've missed a significant part of both your lives. But now that I'm back, I want to be a part of it. I want to know Noor, and I want to make up for the lost time."

Molly felt a surge of frustration. "Ajmal, you can't just waltz back into our lives and expect everything to be as it was. Noor has grown up without you, and I've worked hard to give her a stable and loving environment. I won't let you disrupt that."

He reached out, gently cupping her face, and said, "Molly, I want to be there for both of you. I want to be a family again."

She pulled away, a mix of anger and sadness in her eyes. "Ajmal, you can't make up for the past. Noor doesn't even know you. She doesn't need a stranger claiming to be her father. You left, and we moved on."

Chapter 6

A Royal Proposal.

Ajmal looked at her with a depth of regret in his eyes. "I understand it won't be easy, but I want to try. I want to be a father to Noor."

Molly's emotions were in turmoil, torn between the past and the present. "Ajmal, I need time to think about this. Noor's life is stable now, and I won't let anything disrupt it. Let me talk to her, and we'll decide what's best for her."

He nodded reluctantly, realizing the complexity of the situation. "Take your time, Molly. I just want a chance to be there for both of you."

As they stood near the limo, the tension between them was palpable. Molly knew that whatever decision she made would reshape the course of their lives. She needed to prioritize Noor's well-being and ensure that any rekindling of their past wouldn't bring chaos into the life they had built without him.

"Oh, Mr. Khan, when would I have told you? When you joined Royalty? When you got married? Or when you came to sign your treaty? When, when, and you didn't even guess she is yours after meeting her. So she is only mine. There is no 'we,' only 'I.'

I was with her at the time of the crucial pregnancy. I left my studies, took my hobby as a profession. From birth till now, I did everything for her alone. I delivered her alone. I did all when she was sick or had bad dreams. So please don't come in between us." With that, she pushed him aside and went inside the limo.

Ajmal patted her head. When she looked up, she saw tears in his eyes. He closed the door, saying, "Sorry for not being there when you needed me," and kissed her forehead.

Molly thought the confrontation would make her satisfied, but it didn't. She and Noor slept in late the next morning. Molly made waffles for Noor for breakfast and took her time, enjoying a chat with her daughter. Suddenly, Noor asked, "Mom, how is Aj? When is he coming again? I want to ride in his limo. Mommy, what a car!" Molly was shocked, asking who told her to call him Aj. Noor replied that he did and thanked her for chocolates when they met.

Molly sent Noor off to school and went to the office. In the evening, she received a call from Mrs. Britsm, stating that Noor hadn't come back yet. Angry at Ajmal's actions, Molly rushed to his hotel, leaving her car in the driveway. She was stopped by his guards, but after asserting herself, she was escorted to the poolside.

She saw Ajmal formally dressed by the pool, files on the side table, and Noor swimming with a female guard. Molly's anger dissipated as she saw Noor happily swimming. Noor shouted, "Hi, Mom!" and almost drowned, but Ajmal, fully clothed, jumped into the pool to rescue her. He wrapped her in a towel, rushed her inside, and called for a doctor.

Molly was surprised by Ajmal's actions, who seemed not to listen to her. She thanked him for saving Noor when the nurse took her away. Kneeling beside Noor, Molly asked if she was okay. Ajmal remained by her side, looking at them both.

After Noor left, Molly addressed Ajmal, warning him never to take Noor without informing her. Ajmal gave her a reassuring smile, called his guards, and instructed them not to leave the room without his permission. Molly ran to him, caught his wet collar, and scolded him. Ajmal caught her tightly, asserting that he had every right to spend time with Noor.

As they struggled, Ajmal assured her that no one was leaving. He groaned, buried his head in her neck, teasing her with his nose, and kissed her neck. Without wasting time, he pressed his lips onto hers, whispering that he would take care of them both. His phone ringing interrupted them, and as he pulled away, he promised to return after his duty.

Ajmal went to change, giving Molly a peck before leaving her dazed. He returned, placing another soft kiss on her lips, stating, "We're not alone, Ajmal." He replied, "I don't care," and grabbed her face, smashing his lips on hers, leaving her breathless.

As they entered his other room, all the guards and staff turned towards them. Molly looked at Ajmal, who had a cold face. Everyone bowed as they left the area. In his bedroom, he closed the door, pulled her onto his lap on the nearby recliner, and she gasped. Trying to stand up, he held her tight, whispering, "Don't move."

Running his nose from her neck to her ears, he teased, "You are driving me crazy, love." Before she could reply, someone knocked on the door. She got up, opened the door, and found someone with both their clothes. Taking them, she said thanks and told Ajmal to change. "Okay, love. You change and have snacks with Noor. I will be back in one hour; duty calls," he said before leaving. "Yeah, yeah, yeah," she replied, pointing at the washroom. "Please go and change."

Okay, fine! I will go and change. Oh my God, what is he doing to my heart? URG! This guy is making me absolutely mad. He is not good for my heart and my daughter; we have no match now.

I also went to his dressing room, opened my packet. Wow, from undergarments to socks, a beautiful dark pink one-piece long tunic made of very soft material, and all big brands. Everything was very expensive, but I had no choice, so I wore it. Wow, they fitted so well, and my, I was looking good. There was moisturizer and lipstick too, very thoughtful of whoever brought it.

When I came out, I went straight to Noor, who was in the connecting room, as usual chit-chatting with someone; I could hear her voice.

Noor: Hi, Mom!

Molly went near her, kissed her pumpkin, and said, "Hello, Bebo. Mom was waiting for you." She told one of the staff who was with her to get snacks with a big smile.

"Okay, ma'am," he stepped aside, whispered something on the phone, and went out.

We finished our snacks, and we both were playing knots and crosses when Ajmal came back. Ajmal came and hugged her, "Cupcake, you okay?"

Then he came and stood next to me, lifted my chin, and said, "It's time to tell her, love. Either we do it together, or I will do it on my own. The choice is yours."

She didn't want this. She needed time.

"No."

"When then."

"Soon."

"No. Molly, today and now."

"Are you guys talking about me?" Noor asked.

"Yes, sweetheart. We both have to tell you something very important." Ajmal took Molly's hand firmly. She said, "Pumpkin, remember when you were a small girl, I told you your dad had gone away? I told you I didn't know where he is." Noor nodded, her eyes on her mom. "You see, Bebo, he is Royalty and had to work for his nation. That's why he didn't come, so now his work got over, and he came and found us. It's Ben, isn't it?" She looked at Ben and said, "Can I call you Dad?"

Noor looked at Ajmal with tears in her eyes. Ajmal looked at his crying daughter with heartfelt sadness, and with so much emotion on his face, she looked at her father's eyes searching for a reply. "Yes, sweetheart. Daddy," Noor sobbed. Ajmal hugged her, patting her back, "I know, Pumpkin. This will be hard for you to accept, but I love you, dear, and will make up for all the past years." Noor just cried on his shoulder happily.

Ajmal positioned himself near the chair with his daughter on his lap, looking at her with so much love and warmth. Molly thought about whether she was doing wrong not telling each other about their relationship.

"Okay," she said. "I think we should get back home as we both are tired."

He looked at me with a very charming face. "Afraid to leave her with me?" he said.

"Okay. I didn't want this, but she had no say in this matter as she saw her daughter beaming with happiness. I am tired, Noor. Let's go home. You can meet your dad whenever he is free."

"Done. I will pick up Noor after school. We will both have a ball time tomorrow." Ajmal ruffled Noor's hair and spoke to me. "Noor can't have outside food daily, so you come over and be with Noor the whole day."

"Alright. After 11:30 a.m., I will come," she gave him a big hug and told his assistant to drop them as it was getting late. "But I have my car," she said.

"Go, my driver will drop you. Damn car," he said, giving her an irritated smile.

Noor was so excited. It took me a longer time to make her sleep; she was just chatting about how she would spend the day with her popsy—cooking, shopping, having ice cream, and so on.

The next day, as I was cleaning the kitchen counter,

"Yeahhhh…," I heard Noor jumping and dancing from the doorway, loaded with boxes brought by Ajmal.

"Hey mom, he is here, on time, see," she showed me her hands full. I gave her a smile but gave a very angry glare to Shalik for spoiling her.

Chapter7

Love in the air.

Ajmal was very casually dressed, in beige-colored pants and a blue t-shirt, looking good as always. He gave me a questioning look, wondering why I am angry. "Why so many gifts? Don't spoil her, please," I told him. "You will go away, and I don't want her to get used to all this."

"My sweetest, angry bird," he just hugged me, kissed me, that too in front of my daughter, gave me a heart attack, but this fellow kept on kissing my eyes, cheeks, nose, forehead, and again gave a peck on my lips. "Get it in your head," he said, "I am for keeps from now on. Darling, I am not leaving my family behind. Get it in your head, sweetheart." Looking at us, Noor was clapping and giving thumbs up to his popsy. I was dazed, looking at the father and daughter duo.

I was about to set the table; Ajmal shouted, "Don't set for me, please, as I have already eaten. I will have later on. Noor can have on the kitchen table." "No, love," he told Noor. While he was serving her, he took a bite from Noor's plate. "Wow, dear, this is the world's best pizza, made by my munchkin."

Molly finished her pizza, reached for a soda bottle at the same time as Ajmal did. Their fingers covered hers, they became motionless for a second, looking at each other. Slowly, she drew her hands and poured for everyone. "So, what are your hobbies, Noor?" he asked.

Noor answered, "Drawing, reading stories, dancing, eating lots of cakes and chocolates."

"Oh no, outdoor sports, cycling, basketball, riding horses."

"Oh, I do cycling but never riding."

"I would love a pony, Mom," she looked at her mother and said. "No, dear, not yet," Molly answered.

"Why, Mom?"

Noor asked.

Because riding is expensive, and you are too small, and I find it risky. Noor, but Mom, I want to have pony riding lessons. Ajmal, who was hearing all the conversation between mother and daughter, intervened, "I can pay for her classes; let her go." "No! Thank you. We don't need your money." "Why?" "I will pay for all her lessons when the time is right. She is my princess; she has it in her blood, you will see. We all are good horsemen in our family; some things are genetics. You will, Molly, when Noor will pick up riding, and my doll will have her pony, I will see to it."

Molly: To Noor, "You go to your room, dear." No, Mom, it's so much fun seeing you fighting. She said so innocently. I started laughing. Okay, my little monkey, do what you want. And to Ajmal, she said, "It's not over yet."

Ajmal: He stepped near Molly, gave her a warm hug, kissed her forehead. "Okay, we will decide this later on," he said, looking into my eyes. I nodded, couldn't speak. Even after so many years, his touch gave her tingles. She gets tongue-tied whenever he is near her. His touch affects her so much. Do I still have feelings for him? She should not. After going through so much all alone, how can she bend to him? "Yes, yes, Molly, we will have a discussion tomorrow," he said, "but not in front of Noor." He took her hand in his own and led her towards the living room, making her sit on his lap. She tried to struggle, but he tightened his grip and then made her sit next to him, with fingers inter-twined tightly, he kept his hand on his thighs and said in a commanding voice, "When I started to get up! Sit down, Molly." "Now listen to me without interrupting, we are getting married in two weeks?" "What?" I blinked my brain slowly to process what he is saying. He repeated, "Yes, dear, we are getting married." "No?" I shook my head. With placid calmness, he got up from the sofa and circled around and came to stand in front of me. With his finger, he held my chin, made me look up. Tears burned my eyes and stared at him in shock. His eyes looked down at me in care and love, which I could not believe.

Ajmal: "We will do our duty towards our daughter. She needs both parents, and I apologize for not being there for you when you'd loved needed me the most, dear. But from now, it's my duty to protect you and Noor. Being my princess not only in words but in reality, all her wishes will be fulfilled. And this is called destiny, love; she is born in royalty. So, I can never say no to her for anything; already, she is deprived of my love and care for the past ten years. Is there anything you have not shared, love?" Ajmal pulled out his phone and gave it to me, "Keep this, dear. I can reach you anytime, and even I would love to hear from you. Tomorrow I will change my living arrangements and will let you know. Keep this black card," he gave, "this is for your Noor. Please do shopping without seeing the tags." He said, "As you will have to dress as my queen and princess, and sweetheart less of backless and short dresses as you have to represent royalty when we are going outside. But you can wear anything or nothing also when we are alone." He winked and smiled when telling me these rules and regulations. And last but very important, you will be having one bodyguard always with you. I will appoint one today. After giving me all the instructions, he again kissed me on the forehead. "Okay, love, will be leaving now," and gave me his driver's number, "call him wherever you are going."

After he left, I kept sitting on the sofa for how long, even I didn't know. I had no romance left in me, no illusion of what this marriage will be like. Is it nothing, just an alliance between us for our daughter? I kept thinking. Do I still love him?

Chapter 8

Mix Up Feelings

Molly: It was childish, but I kept myself from my work, switched off my phone, didn't eat food, tried reading, watching movies, but was not able to do anything. Ajmal's words kept coming to me. My future was at stake. There was no one I could ask. We were totally opposite now. I knew nothing about his nation, his lifestyle, his family. What about my job? All these unknown fears were bothering me. The knock on my door startled me. "Mom, I am home," Noor shouted, swinging her hair. She gave me a lethargic smile. "Mom, I am so tired and hungry," jumps on my bed upside down. "Hi, love," I called the caretaker to give her a milkshake, then food. "Mom, we are going shopping, hurrayyyyyy." "Who told you that, dear?" "Who else, Mom? Popsyyyy……" I froze for a second. "What kind of shopping?" I asked. "Your wedding dress and mine, bridesmaid, and lots of parties, which will be held after the wedding, Mom," she told me.

Aren't you happy, Mom? She asked, looking worried. "Of course, dear, but I am a little nervous; that's why you are getting that feeling." She jumps and started playing with the ball.

And, Mom, don't buy frilly stuff. We will get elegant and classy dresses seen in Vogue magazine. "You will look so beautiful when you will walk down the aisle." I kept staring at her at what she said so innocently. "Okies, Mom, I will play with PlayStation; Stephie must be coming any time," with that, she left me dazed. That very time I saw move in with ice cream tubs in his hands, with our favorite flavors.

After placing the ice cream tubs in the refrigerator, he came and sat next to me. Before he could say anything, I addressed him, "Look Ajmal, we don't have to get married. Now you know where I live, and your father is also no more, so you will have no problem coming and meeting me and your daughter. Now, with no secrets between us, do you understand what I am saying?"

"Are you doing this for your daughter?" I asked. "You can visit her anytime. I will not stop you!"

He looked at me with his sweetest, idiotic smile, which always stirred something within me. "Sweetheart, you are not understanding. I have missed her first ten years of her life and missed you also terribly. So I want to do this right this time, love." With that, his mouth lowered to hers. Molly wanted to resist, but her body betrayed her; she responded instantly to his touch, delightfully. She threaded her fingers in his dark hair. For a moment, she felt like a teenager again; she was drowning in his kisses.

He eased her back gently, tracing his fingers on her lips and smiling at her. She flushed, looking at him. "I am going to play with Noor, with her new video game which I had promised her, dear, so I must leave you." I nodded my head, unable to speak due to the intense emotions coursing through my body. "I have a function to attend this weekend. After that, I am free; my all free time is for my daughter and you, dear."

Molly watched him leave, entered Noor's room, and contemplated the sanctity of marriage. Something that should not be forced or rushed, yet he desired a quick marriage. Ten years of a void between them, something he failed to comprehend. Having lived a playboy life, mingling with models and actresses, even his wife was one. How would she compare to those elegant, classy females he had been with? Molly, a simple sweet girl and a devoted mother, questioned her ability to cope with his lifestyle, new to her. The fact that he had not consulted her, making such a significant decision about a crucial aspect of her life, left her bewildered.

Approaching their room later, she saw his gaze pierce into her eyes, searching her soul. He knew her too well. His firm jaw, unshaved since the day before last, showcased a sun-kissed skin, a perfect contrast to hers.

"Hello, Pumpkin!" I said, enjoying?

"Yeah, Mom, come on; Dad is leaving soon." I was surprised at my daughter calling Ajmal by different endearments every time.

After bidding us goodbye, he left. It was a very long day for me, contemplating the future ahead. In the morning, I left early with pending work, already having called Mrs. Brisban to be with Noor for the whole day. Entering the office, everyone was smiling and congratulating me. I was zapped and surprised at their reactions, even from people who didn't like me, all giving me smiles. Entering the cabin, there he was, sitting in his Armani suit, looking like a Greek God, surrounded by my assistants, other executives, and, of course, my partner, who gave me dirty looks. Ajmal watched her with a crooked grin, got up, wrapped his arms around my waist, and kissed my forehead. He liked kissing my forehead, doing it at least two to three times a day when he is near me. Honestly, I don't know how I got to the chair near my table and sat down. Of all people, I had to see him in my office, with my secret out, visible to all my colleagues.

"So, sweetheart, I have told them you will be leaving Senetal and would be joining my office soon, after marriage." A murmur rippled through the entire cabin, and I folded my arms, leaning back to observe bobbing heads. When nobody made a move, Ajmal twitches his lips at everyone's reactions. Ajmal's head rotated slowly until his eyes met mine; he could see daggers coming out from my eyes. Gazing at him, he commanded me to follow his orders. To everybody, it seemed we were looking, gazing lovingly into each other's eyes. The murmur increased inside the office; I heard the sharp intake of breaths from people. Electricity charged the air. Ajmal gave a dark look and said, "I will call you." His shoulders were hunched, eyes filled with wisdom, as if they had seen things he must not voice out. He came very near me, hugged me, and said in my ear, "I am doing this because I love you." I hoped this works well and made it easy for you to make the announcement. With that, he left, bidding farewell to everyone. When he was gone, I knew I would have to answer them.

"So, will you elaborate, Your Majesty?" Ric asked me. "Such a big secret you withheld from me, from me, your partner and friend," he shouted when everybody vacated from my office. I should have guessed at the conference, when you came back suddenly, leaving me behind. "Oh, how I apologized to him, and then he congratulated me."

Ajmal called up Molly and told her to be ready in the evening, as they would be having an evening out. Molly, proving more stubborn, made him realize how much he had missed her. He had missed seeing her pregnant with his child, missed seeing her nursing their baby, not knowing anything about Noor. He was determined to make up for it; it was his duty, and he would convince his stubborn Molly.

He had just two weeks left before he had to return home and begin work on his new treaty. He didn't plan to return home alone, and before he left, he had to convince Molly to join him.

"That dress is pretty, Mom," Noor said when Molly came out from her room. The deep rose long dress with a flowing skirt around her hips made her look very pretty. She looked like a model, a fact of which she was unaware. It boosted her confidence, making her realize the proverb "clothes make the man" suited her.

When the doorbell rang, Noor ran to open it and greeted him with a sweet smile. Despite not knowing her relation with him, she secretly hoped he was her dad. Ajmal gave Noor her present.

"A present? What?" Molly protested. He merely smiled, took out a delicate chain with a small diamond heart, and made Noor wear it.

"Thank you, Popsy. It's so pretty."

"And this is for you," he came closer to Molly, took her wrist, and adorned her with a shimmering ruby and diamond bracelet.

"From me to you, dear."

"Oh, Aj, I can't take diamonds."

"Why not? It's just like accepting flowers. Indulge me, honey. Take it without saying anything, please."

"Thank you! I will always cherish it."

"Okay, honey, let's go."

Salid stood by the limousine when Ajmal and Molly emerged from the house. He opened the doors for them and politely greeted Molly. Salid was coming with them as a bodyguard.

"We are going to a concert. Like us, he is also a music lover," Ajmal informed her.

The Kennedy Center was crowded when they reached, and they were made to sit with the senator. The young wife of the senator became friendly with Molly, and they were chit-chatting in no time. They enjoyed the music, and after ages, Ajmal felt carefree. Molly was like a breath of fresh air in his life, and he thanked Allah for that.

Molly asked him why he needed bodyguards always. "It's more than a necessity; it's our tradition from many generations, and for our own safety too," he said, lacing his fingers through hers and linking her hands to his thighs, resting them against his hard muscles.

The music was beautiful, the acoustics perfect for the delightful enjoyment of the orchestra's rendition of classical music. Molly began to relax with the music. After the show, they thanked the senator and left for his hotel.

In the limo heading for the hotel, Molly asked Ajmal about Manasia, wondering if it was all desert, as depicted in movies. He chuckled softly, describing the beautiful country with a variety of topography, from the shores of the Mediterranean to the dunes of the Sahara Desert, with a few scattered oases. Their villa, he mentioned, was near the sea bank with a private beach.

"It sounds nice." Molly woke with a start to see Ajmal waking her up softly. Her hands were over his chest, and she was almost in his lap. Embarrassed and unsure when she had fallen asleep, she remembered he was telling her about Manasia. Her heart pounded fast, thinking about Salid witnessing this. Embarrassed and turning red, Ajmal kissed her. She slowly withdrew her hands and got out of the limo, as he told her to come for some time.

When they reached his room, he took her in his arms again. "You will like my home, Molly. My villa is large with lots of glass to give an outdoor feel. We have roses and bougainvillea flowers all over the house, date palms on all boundaries, with a very big yard, swings, and a pool. It's a very appropriate place for Noor's upbringing. Do you have pictures of your home?"

"No, dear, you will have to wait until we go there."

"We are not going there, Ajmal," Molly said hastily.

"You and Noor are coming, and that is final, dear. The sooner you accept it, the easier it will be for all of us."

"Did you enjoy the symphony, love?" he immediately changed the topic.

"Yes, it was wonderful." She felt like she was plunging into his eyes, and it turned out to be such a magical night, love in the air. Even when he lowered his head, she couldn't move. Liquid heat was getting into her body, his touch provoking sensational feelings. The soft caressing of his thumbs against her cheeks gave her shivers. Drowning in his deep kisses, she was embarrassed when the bell on the door interrupted them, and Salid came with an eatables trolley.

"Come, supper awaits," he guided them to his suite. Megan avoided Salid's eyes, knowing he must have seen them kissing and feeling shy. "I need to go home, Aj," Molly said.

"Come, I have had dinner prepared for us. So eat, and then I will drop you. Stay and enjoy."

She stepped into his suite, her hair packed in a low loose bun with nude lip gloss. Unaware of how enchanting she looked, Ajmal just stared at her from his end, smiling, thinking she was his and his only. Allah had been kind to him, giving him her as his love and her precious daughter as well. He knew he had to convince her more.

She's in a justifiable position, thrust into his world with all its status and required to leave her comfort zone to accompany him to a new place within a tight twenty-day timeframe. This is because he needs to return home, and he can't risk her leaving now, especially with Noor. She might not fully comprehend her role as a queen and Noor's status as his little princess. Leaving them without proper security is not an option. Given her status as a billionaire's wife, she needs to maintain a certain image.

As dinner was arranged, we awaited the serving of the courses. We began with appetizers, engaged in conversation, and later reminisced about our college days. Moving on to the main course, a silence settled between us as we finished our food.

I requested red wine, knowing her preference for red over white wine. It was delightful, and I happily consumed its content, even asking for more, although she was content with just one glass.

We engaged in a conversation about my country and new business opportunities. I asked for her input on various business ideas, as I believed that every woman has an entrepreneurial spirit, something I learned from my mother. While I've encountered many models and actresses in my social circles, Molly stood out as different. She embodied both intelligence and beauty, much like my mother and my sisters-in-law, who are involved in various projects for the welfare of our nation. I aspired to see Molly at the pinnacle, helping me as an advisor, a friend, and a partner in both business and love.

"Do you have any business ideas in mind, my love?"

She responded, "The ideas came to me as we were talking," nodding her head. "You're passionate about uplifting women in your country," she continued. As we maintained eye contact, I was entranced by the way she listened to me. Her insights filled my heart with joy. She suggested ideas such as establishing a fashion house, becoming a designer focused on Muslim traditions, venturing into the toy-making industry, and supporting children's welfare. I felt blessed to have her as my future partner.

After dinner, I shifted her chair, and together we moved from the dining area to the living room. However, just before we made the transition, my phone beeped. I reached into my pocket, and I saw a private name on the screen. I nodded to her, indicating that it was a private call, and she sat down near the fireplace.

Molly was engrossed in admiring the robotics plants within the room, and her gaze eventually fell on the library, neatly arranged on one wall. This was something that we shared in common: our love for books. She enjoyed reading books and preferred romantic novels. Since she had no interest in having boyfriends, she found solace in the fantasy of the romantic worlds within the books she read.

Molly wondered about the kind of women I typically associated with. She considered that people like me usually preferred smart, classy women who excelled in various fields. They often socialized with billionaires' daughters. She questioned why I had chosen her over others, expressing her desire for a man like me who would place a ring on her finger.

While sitting in one corner of my room as I attended the phone call, Molly questioned her thoughts. She wondered whether I was genuinely interested in her as I claimed every day. Her mind drifted into these contemplations, and she hesitated to leave the corner, fearing that I might view it as an invasion of my privacy.

Stepping onto the extended balcony filled with lush plants, Molly felt the evening air brushing her face. Grateful that her hair was securely held in a bun, she basked in the refreshing breeze, feeling a sense of tranquility. She inhaled deeply, savoring the fresh air.

But Ajmal, with an unsatisfied tone, abruptly questioned her presence on the balcony. He reminded her that she should not go anywhere without bodyguards. Molly responded curtly, defending her need to enjoy the fresh air. Her harsh words and defiance caught Ajmal's attention, and he gazed at her with icy intensity. As their eyes met, he advised her not to behave like a child.

To her surprise, Ajmal took hold of her hand and led her back inside. The close proximity intensified their connection, and before she knew it, he pulled her into his arms and kissed her with an unwavering passion. The kiss was deep, stirring up a mixture of excitement and vulnerability within Molly.

Ajmal confessed his desire for her as his future wife, promising to do things the right way by marrying her first. He even suggested that they inform her father. Molly declared her love and interest in him, appreciating his words. The passionate kiss they shared left a lasting impact on both of them.

For Ajmal, that explosive kiss left him reflecting on what he had done. He hoped Molly hadn't been frightened by the intensity of the moment. He realized that he was losing control every time he was near her and felt a magnetic fascination for her. He also recognized the paramount importance of having her in his life, as she and Noor were his lifelines.

For Molly, that evening had turned into an unexpectedly romantic date. She felt herself falling for Ajmal all over again, and her perception of him and his lifestyle was changing.

She would need to acclimate to his lifestyle if she decided to give him a chance. Casually glancing at him, he responded with a tantalizing smile that had the power to make her head spin. His gentle caress on her nose accompanied a question.

"Can I ask you something?" he inquired.

Curiously, she responded, "What is it?"

"Why didn't you go to university to finish your degree? If you want to finish, we can apply in our hometown, dear," he suggested, catching her off guard.

"I'll let you know once I've made up my mind," she replied, not wanting to reveal the burdens of responsibilities and the mental trauma she had faced during the time when he was not there, and she had to navigate through challenges alone.

The prospect of a new beginning and potential marriage lingered in her thoughts. Noor, her daughter, inquired about her evening with Ajmal, and Molly shared the news that he wanted to marry her soon. Noor, intrigued, asked about Molly's decision, to which she responded with a non-committal "Let's see."

As the morning unfolded, Noor greeted her with curiosity about her first drive and dinner with Ajmal. It seemed like fate was giving her another chance at love. Noor, sensing the importance of the moment, asked about Molly's decision regarding Ajmal's proposal.

Later, when Molly entered the office, she was met with peculiar greetings from the staff. A senior staff member questioned why she was present at the office instead of having office-related matters handled at home. Perplexed by the unexpected warmth, Molly was taken to the office of a senior executive who expressed surprise that she hadn't informed them earlier about her uncomfortable workload.

The revelation came when the executive disclosed that Ajmal had informed the company about their impending wedding. The news spread quickly, and Molly found herself being congratulated on her wedding. The director of the company, a high-end figure, personally congratulated her as well. Although surprised by the attention, she felt a new wave of emotions as she was addressed as "future Mrs. Sheikh Ajmal S."

Despite her request to return to work, Molly was informed that Mr. Ajmal would be upset if she did so. They assured her that they would handle her pending tasks. At home, Molly watched a press conference where Ajmal revealed details about their private life, including hints about their upcoming wedding. Unable to bear more, she turned off the TV and called her father to share the news.

The next day, she was instructed to be ready for shopping with Ajmal. Despite having a perfect night of dreams reminiscent of a fairy tale, she woke up to the reality of preparing for the day. Anticipating sophistication, she chose a chocolate-brown dress that exuded daring yet sophisticated vibes with its fitted bodice, pencil-thin skirt, and a tasteful slit. The day unfolded with expectations, bringing her closer to a future that was both exciting and uncertain.

At least the dress covered her whole body, though it outlined every curve. Her hair cascaded down her back, straight and loosely brushed. She opted for light makeup—brown eyeshadow, a touch of mascara, and peach-colored lip gloss, leaving her feeling satisfied, good, and fresh. This day marked the first time she accepted the relationship, a realization that dawned on her while getting ready.

Chapter 9

Preprations.

However, her newfound confidence waned as Ajmal's warm gaze slid over her, assessing her slowly. Under his intense gaze, she blushed like a young girl and turned beetroot in color. Ajmal, in blue trousers and a white shirt, emanated an attractive aura of male dominance. Moving closer, he held her chin, wrapped his arms around her waist, and pulled her close.

A gasp escaped her lips as their eyes met, and their lips brushed against each other. His experienced lips tenderly moved, deepening the kiss, and after a moment, he pulled away. The lingering question of whether it was love or mere desire crossed her mind.

Ajmal stepped back, but his hand remained on her waist, reluctant to let go. They walked down, arm in arm, showcasing their happiness to Noor, who had earlier harbored doubts about their relationship. The couple walked confidently towards the limo, with heads held high, where Noor awaited with Salid.

In the limo, Ajmal's strong gaze focused on her, making her feel as small as an ant. He praised her beauty, expressing his desire to know her fully and have her love. Molly reciprocated by giving him a peck on the lips but retreated, not wanting Noor to witness their intimate moment.

As they proceeded with their shopping, Ajmal planned lunch at his hotel, revealing that it was his last day there, and he intended to get a villa for around twenty days. At a prestigious boutique, he was captivated by Molly trying on various outfits. Unable to decide, he instructed to pack all the outfits, matching sandals, bags, and even undergarments from Victoria's Secret, just as he did for Noor.

After Noor left with her shopping, Molly felt a sense of relief. At the hotel, as they entered their suite, Molly walked ahead, still confused about the impending marriage. Ajmal, understanding her thoughts, took her aside, expressing his intentions for marriage and providing a legitimate family for their child, addressing her financial concerns. He leaned in for a kiss on her forehead, an affectionate gesture, before kissing her lips with a blend of carnal desire.

As Molly moved away, Ajmal thought about proving to her that his love and care would be enough for her and Noor. After completing their shopping, they returned to the hotel, where Ajmal expressed his desire to talk while enjoying refreshments. Molly, still uncertain about marriage, shared her past, including her friendships, freelance work, and odd jobs to make ends meet. Ajmal, empathetic, apologized for not being there during her challenging times and inquired about why she didn't seek her father's help.

The mention of her father brought back embarrassing memories, and Molly turned red with shame and anger. Ajmal, sensing her distress, offered a glass of water and reassured her. He expressed understanding of her past and suggested they forget about it. Before Molly could resist, he pulled her into his arms, kissing her passionately. In an attempt to alleviate his regret, she reciprocated with soft kisses, sharing a moment that seemed to mend the pain he held for her.

She gently placed her hand against Ajmal's mouth, quieting him. "No, Ajmal, don't hurt yourself. I'm sorry for dredging up mud from the past. It's over, dear. Life always comes with problems; that's the way it is. We will learn to solve them together." He smiled, slid his arms around her neck, and agreed, "Yes, dear, there are possibilities. We will do that," inching his mouth closer.

Sensing that giving in to a kiss would mean agreeing to anything, she pulled back. Ajmal stepped away, abruptly changing his mood, almost flattening her with the shift.

Ajmal was left stunned by the passion she had ignited with just one kiss. He desired her in every way, and even the thought of how she felt in his arms was enough to stir him. Apologizing for his proud and stubborn nature, he confessed to commanding decisions without consulting her. He expressed his love for both her and Noor, emphasizing that if fate had brought them together after so long, it was meant to be.

Molly reassured him, "I understand," as he placed his hand on the small of her back, leading her through the hotel lobby. As the elevator doors opened, he left her with a swift, hard kiss on her mouth, saying, "Until the day after tomorrow. I have to wind up a lot of things tomorrow."

Ajmal, after sending Molly off, sat on an armchair with his eyes closed. His thoughts drifted back to when his father had instructed him to carry on the family's legacy. He recalled his father's words, emphasizing the responsibilities that came with wealth and power and the need to follow rules for the nation. His marriage was predestined, an arranged one, but it had not brought happiness. The stark contrast between his first marriage and Molly's nature lingered in his memories.

The next morning, Molly woke up to the sound of the alarm. After a quick shower, she got ready in jeans and a simple top and prepared breakfast for Noor and herself. Promising Noor to make her favorite chocolate chip cookies, Molly began her day.

Noor, excited for her popsy's visit to school, struggled to find her hair tie. Ajmal received a call from his mother, offering heartfelt congratulations and informing him about the return date as preparations for the couple's party were underway.

Molly went about her chores and completed some work that had been sent home by Ric. Reflecting on her journey from college to her current job in Washington, she acknowledged her luck when her work was recognized by AP and UPL, leading her to Senetel. Last night, Ajmal had asked her about liking Washington, and she had expressed her fondness for the place.

As Molly finished her chores, she pondered over Ajmal's persistent persuasion for her to consider living in Manasia. He argued that it was a place she hadn't seen yet and promised not to leave them behind after the wedding. Despite his convincing efforts, Molly remained firm in her decision not to go there.

For the past two days, there had been no news from Ajmal. No calls or messages. Despite the desire to reach out, her ego held her back. In the evening, after Noor was occupied with swimming and cycling, Molly found herself making coffee. The doorbell rang unexpectedly, and to her surprise, it was Ajmal at the door.

In that moment, she forgot every reason they argued. Rushing into his arms, they shared a bear hug, and as they entered the living room, the tension melted away.

She gently placed her hand against Ajmal's mouth, quieting him. "No, Ajmal, don't hurt yourself. I'm sorry for dredging up mud from the past. It's over, dear. Life always comes with problems; that's the way it is. We will learn to solve them together." He smiled, slid his arms around her neck, and agreed, "Yes, dear, there are possibilities. We will do that," inching his mouth closer.

Sensing that giving in to a kiss would mean agreeing to anything, she pulled back. Ajmal stepped away, abruptly changing his mood, almost flattening her with the shift.

Ajmal was left stunned by the passion she had ignited with just one kiss. He desired her in every way, and even the thought of how she felt in his arms was enough to stir him. Apologizing for his proud and stubborn nature, he confessed to commanding decisions without consulting her. He expressed his love for both her and Noor, emphasizing that if fate had brought them together after so long, it was meant to be.

Molly reassured him, "I understand," as he placed his hand on the small of her back, leading her through the hotel lobby. As the elevator doors opened, he left her with a swift, hard kiss on her mouth, saying, "Until the day after tomorrow. I have to wind up a lot of things tomorrow."

Ajmal, after sending Molly off, sat on an armchair with his eyes closed. His thoughts drifted back to when his father had instructed him to carry on the family's legacy. He recalled his father's words, emphasizing the responsibilities that came with wealth and power and the need to follow rules for the nation. His marriage was predestined, an arranged one, but it had not brought happiness. The stark contrast between his first marriage and Molly's nature lingered in his memories.

The next morning, Molly woke up to the sound of the alarm. After a quick shower, she got ready in jeans and a simple top and prepared breakfast for Noor and herself. Promising Noor to make her favorite chocolate chip cookies, Molly began her day.

Noor, excited for her popsy's visit to school, struggled to find her hair tie. Ajmal received a call from his mother, offering heartfelt congratulations and informing him about the return date as preparations for the couple's party were underway.

Molly went about her chores and completed some work that had been sent home by Ric. Reflecting on her journey from college to her current job in Washington, she acknowledged her luck when her work was recognized by AP and UPL, leading her to Senetel. Last night, Ajmal had asked her about liking Washington, and she had expressed her fondness for the place.

As Molly finished her chores, she pondered over Ajmal's persistent persuasion for her to consider living in Manasia. He argued that it was a place she hadn't seen yet and promised not to leave them behind after the wedding. Despite his convincing efforts, Molly remained firm in her decision not to go there.

For the past two days, there had been no news from Ajmal. No calls or messages. Despite the desire to reach out, her ego held her back. In the evening, after Noor was occupied with swimming and cycling, Molly found herself making coffee. The doorbell rang unexpectedly, and to her surprise, it was Ajmal at the door.

In that moment, she forgot every reason they argued. Rushing into his arms, they shared a bear hug, and as they entered the living room, the tension melted away.

Their heat pulsed in unison, and she wished she could grasp the moment forever, not thinking beyond it. He laid her back against his arm. "Molly," he said, "you have to choose your wedding dress or wedding rings. Let's go tomorrow and choose."

"We will go tomorrow," she replied. He kissed her goodbye and left. Molly lay under the covers, wide awake. Despite her hectic schedule, it had never happened before that she felt uncomfortable in her own bed. In her heart of hearts, she knew it was due to the conversation with Ajmal the previous night, which had shaken her.

The Caller ID made her roll her eyes for a second—it was her father. "Hey, Dad," she uttered. "How are you, sweetie?" he asked. Molly shared everything that happened the previous night. Her father, a middle-aged man with an average height, a light complexion, and a heart of gold, listened. She remembered how she used to confide in him about every small incident. Even now, that habit continued, and she poured out the details of her conversation with Ajmal.

Molly thought about the significance of getting engaged, a momentous occasion that marks the start of a new chapter and a full-time promise. The morning coffee in her kitchen had her contemplating the sacred nature of marriage, the second most important relationship in a woman's life. How would she survive in this new life with different people and traditions?

Just then, a call from Ajmal's assistant informed her about the pickup time. In his room, Ajmal took out his wallet and stopped on a picture of a beautiful girl—blonde hair, ocean blue eyes, sharp cheeks—his Molly. He desired her, feeling himself drowning in her warmth. He mused on her perfection and how marrying her could be his own heaven.

Noor interrupted Molly's thoughts, asking about the timing to get ready. Molly answered, and soon they were on their way.

At the bridal boutique, Ajmal surprised them with VIP treatment and an array of designer gowns for Molly and Noor. Molly was dumbfounded by the exquisite choices. One gown, in particular, took her breath away—perfect fit, in a satin-onion pink color, adorned with ivory thread, pearl seed beads, and a neckline with Swarovski crystals.

Looking at Ajmal, she felt a wave of warmth and love. It seemed as if he could see through her, all the way to the depth of her soul. After finalizing her gown, she changed, and Ajmal selected evening wear dresses, shoes, bags, and cosmetics for both her and Noor. They left the boutique, and Ajmal treated them to Café Allegro, the best coffee shop in Seattle, with a private cabin filled with toasts, cakes, different varieties of coffee, and more. Noor grinned away, enjoying the spread.

Ajmal asked Noor, "So what do you think of your shopping, dear?"

"Fabulous, Dad," she exclaimed. Glancing at Ajmal, she thought about how fortunate she was to marry him.

"Are we done here?" Ajmal asked when they finished their coffee.

"Yeah," Noor replied.

As they settled into the limo, Ajmal noticed Molly's quiet demeanor. "Hope you're okay. You looked gorgeous in the gown," he said, kissing her softly.

Since the night they had chosen their wedding clothes, Ajmal had been showering them with dates, gifts, and his loving presence. Both Molly and Noor had become addicted to his affection, finding joy in being with him.

Molly was currently at the office on-site, working on a presentation due the next day. She was engrossed in her work when Ajmal surprised her. "You shouldn't work too hard, sweetheart," he said, kissing her. He brought refreshments and suggested she take a break.

Ajmal kissed her again and promised to wait outside while she finished her work and had a sandwich. Later, in his limo, he took her to the park where they had their first date during college. To her surprise, the place was decorated with lights, fresh flowers, a cake on the small center table, and rose petals scattered on the ground. It was a beautiful setup, and Molly expressed her delight with a tip-toe peck on his lips.

A week since they had chosen their wedding clothes, Ajmal declared his love for Molly. He spoke of their forced marriage being the best thing that happened in his life. On bended knee, he presented a solitaire ring and proposed to her. Overwhelmed with joy, Molly enthusiastically said yes, and they embraced.

Molly expressed her desire to start their relationship as lovers before getting married. Gazing into his eyes, she drew him close, and they shared a passionate kiss that intensified quickly. Lost in the moment, Molly crossed her hands over his neck, but the kiss was abruptly interrupted.

After cutting the cake and sharing a glass of wine, they chatted for a while. Ajmal then suggested leaving, and Molly leaned into his embrace in the limo. Their moment was shattered by a phone call. After a conversation in Arabic, Ajmal looked at Molly and said he had to go back to Manasia due to trouble at home. He assured her of their safety, leaving strict instructions not to step out alone.

When they reached home, Sadik, Ajmal's bodyguard, kept a watchful eye, and Ajmal bid them goodbye. Molly felt a mix of emotions as he kissed her softly, assuring her of their future together. As Ajmal left, Molly contemplated the political situation in his nation and the role she might play in his affairs.

Molly and Noor slept in late the next morning. Molly prepared waffles, boiled eggs, and coffee for breakfast. They enjoyed their meal, chatting about the previous day's shopping. Molly shared details about Ajmal's family and Manasia, sparking Noor's interest in visiting.

Excitedly, Noor asked if she could visit her friend Stephie for a bike ride. Molly agreed but reminded her to tidy her room. Aware of the need for caution, Molly called the guards to inform them of Noor's movements.

After her second cup of lemon tea, Molly contemplated cleaning her room, as the house help had not arrived. Suddenly, the phone rang; it was Ric. He inquired about the protests in Manasia, and Molly confirmed that Ajmal had left due to the unrest. Ric promised to send her a copy of the news.

Later that day, Molly felt increasingly uneasy. She tried calling Ajmal but found his number busy. Her worry escalated as she spoke to Salid, who mentioned Ajmal being in a meeting.

Chatper 10

Accident.

Despite Noor's cheerful chatter about her day, Molly remained distressed. That night, sleep eluded her as she thought about Noor's disappointment over not receiving a call from Ajmal. Ric's late-night call brought alarming news – the hotel where Ajmal stayed was on fire. The gravity of the situation sank in.

Ric assured Molly they would pick her up, and she quickly prepared herself. Before leaving, she instructed the bodyguards to watch over Noor. As they approached the hotel, the growing flames became more visible. Police barricades surrounded the area, but Molly, driven by desperation, broke through, running toward the burning building.

The scene was horrifying – the top floors were engulfed in flames, and the heat was intense. Molly prayed for Ajmal's safety. At the police barrier, she hesitated for a moment, but unable to bear the sight of her love burning, she ran towards the building. Ignoring warnings and pleas to return, she witnessed people being evacuated, some coughing heavily, and others on stretchers.

In a state of panic, Molly prayed fervently for Ajmal's safety, begging for his well-being in the midst of the unfolding tragedy.

The fear of losing Ajmal consumed Molly. As she approached the burning hotel, she desperately sought information about Ajmal's whereabouts. Firefighters, engrossed in rescue efforts, could not provide her with any news. Ric offered comfort, assuring her that Ajmal, being a tough man, would likely be okay.

Amidst the chaos, a paramedic emerged with an injured man. Molly recognized Salid, Ajmal's confidant, and sought answers about Ajmal's whereabouts. Salid, visibly distressed, couldn't provide clarity, blaming the dense smoke inside. He urged Molly to go to the hospital, assuring her that an ambulance was waiting.

Arriving at the hospital, Molly anxiously awaited news about Ajmal. When he was brought in, barely conscious and covered in burns, Molly felt a mix of relief and worry. Determined to stay by his side, she insisted on accompanying him in the ambulance.

As Ajmal was admitted, Molly, now Mrs. Ajmal Bin Shallik, filled out forms with pride. The nurse suggested shifting him to a private ward, to which Molly affirmed his capability to afford it. Salid, also admitted, was to be placed in a private ward adjacent to Ajmal's.

After completing the paperwork, the nurse updated Molly on Ajmal's condition. Despite severe injuries, he was stable. Molly, overwhelmed with love, stood by his bedside, holding his hand. Ajmal, awakening to her touch, expressed feeling "never ever better." Their exchange of affectionate words continued, with Molly noting his heroism in Manasia.

Ajmal, playful even in his weakened state, assured Molly of chartering a plane for their wedding ceremony and accommodating her family as royal guests in Manasia. He promised to arrange everything for Noor's schooling and invited Molly to return whenever she pleased. In the hospital room, amidst the beeping machines, Molly and Ajmal shared a moment of tenderness, looking forward to a future filled with love and understanding.

So, my dearest Molly, will you marry this not-so-perfect man who will love you forever?

Molly replied, "It is I who would be honored to be your wife, Your Highness." She sealed her words with a soft kiss. "I've loved you for ten years, dear. I tried to forget you, but could not."

Ajmal, holding her hands, responded, "And I loved you, dear."

Before moving on, Ajmal made special invitations for Noor's friend Stephie and her parents, as well as Ric and his family and team for the marriage coverage.

Ajmal acknowledged the significance of the moment, stating, "This is a rebirth, and I don't want any unhappiness. What is life after death, I had experienced a few hours back. Sweetheart, the past is behind and gone. There is nothing we can do to change. Let's look forward. From today, we will start our life with utmost joy and happiness."

Molly agreed, "Yes, dear. Now please sleep for some time to ease your pain. I know you are subsiding it." She ran her fingers through his hair, comforting him.

Upon waking up, Ajmal inquired about Salid and Noor, expressing his desire for their well-being. Molly assured him that she would speak to the doctors for an early discharge. Ajmal, back to his commanding self, playfully issued orders, and Molly, now a queen, reminded him that he couldn't order his queen. They shared a tender moment, affirming their commitment to a life filled with love.

Later, Molly waited as a team of doctors examined Ajmal and Salid. Ric returned with clothes for Molly, and he informed her about the media coverage surrounding them.

When she entered Ajmal's room after changing, he noted her exhaustion and insisted that she rest. Molly, not fully agreeing, was kissed on the forehead by Ajmal. He playfully ordered her to leave and start packing, hinting at their imminent departure for Manasia.

Late morning, Molly returned home, where Noor, initially upset, was comforted by Molly's assurance that Ajmal was fine. They decided to visit him in the evening.

At the hospital, they were surprised by increased security. Noor, overwhelmed with joy, hugged Ajmal tightly. In the evening, she prepared a "get well soon" card for him. Upon entering the hospital, they were surrounded by guards who led them to Ajmal's room.

Noor, excitedly chattering away, was embraced by Ajmal, and tears of joy filled his eyes. As the father-daughter duo shared a heartwarming moment, Noor curiously asked about a royal wedding. Ajmal explained the significance with pride.

Meanwhile, Ric informed Molly that news channels were covering Ajmal, and their pictures were everywhere. The events marked the beginning of a new chapter in their lives.

Chapter 11

The Grand Wedding.

At that moment, I witnessed Ajmal standing before me, holding a beautiful tray with an open box. Inside was the most exquisite sapphire ring, approximately ten carats, surrounded by ten solitaires. Ajmal took my hand, placed the ring on my finger, and declared, "Now you are officially my queen." He embraced me, kissed my forehead, and Noor joined in the celebration, clapping and dancing in joy.

After leaving the hospital, a few guards assisted us with packing. We took along new belongings, including some of my cashmere hoodies and jackets. Following an exhausting flight, we finally arrived in Manasia. We traveled in separate cars to the palace, surrounded by guards. The drive was long and silent, with only Noor's chit-chat breaking the silence. Reporters captured the scene as we approached the palace, and the realization set in that they would now be constantly under public scrutiny.

Before reaching Manasia, both Noor and I received makeovers on the flight. We were groomed, dressed in new outfits, and looked classy. The female guards accompanied us in the limo. Upon reaching the beautiful castle with gardens and a grand entrance, we were greeted by a well-dressed man who informed us of the king's presence. Ajmal's grandmother welcomed us warmly, picked up Noor, and led us into a room adorned with light pink walls, chandeliers, Persian rugs, and elegant silverware. Ajmal's mother assured me that my future was secure, encouraging me to treat the castle as my own home.

Eventually, we were shown to our part of the castle—an expansive apartment with impeccable interiors, equipped with everything Noor could desire. When Ajmal came to meet us, I closed the distance between us, giving him a warm hug and a peck on the lips. He briefed us about the arrangements for the guests and informed us that we would not be meeting until the wedding. Dazed by the unfolding events, I was left contemplating the whirlwind of changes in my life.

As I prepared for the wedding, my father stood behind me, offering last-minute touches. He expressed his happiness for me and reminded me of the responsibilities that would come with royalty. The nervousness kicked in, but my father reassured me, emphasizing that Ajmal would likely feel the same.

Walking down the aisle with my father, I felt my heart racing as the chapel, beautifully adorned with exotic flowers and lights, opened up before us. The wedding planner signaled us to start walking to the music of "Marry Me" by Jason Derulo. Amid smiles from friends and family, I reached Ajmal at the altar, and my father handed my hand to him. We exchanged vows, and when I declared myself the happiest bride, I saw love, warmth, and happiness in Ajmal's eyes.

Our warmth continued as we shared our first kiss, and the crowd erupted in cheers and applause. I faced the crowd, smiling, and declared, "I'm now Mrs. Sheikh Ajmal Bin Shallik!" After the ceremony, my mother-in-law handed us a package for a honeymoon in the Maldives.

The Maldives turned out to be a true gem in the Indian Ocean, a natural wonderland. As I stole glances at my husband, the reality of my honeymoon hit me, and my cheeks turned red. I looked at the church's altar, silently praying for guidance.

Ajmal approached, complimenting me on my wedding dress and calling me his queen. Overwhelmed, I couldn't take my eyes off him, recalling the priest's final words before he carried me to the reception.

In the reception, the audience cheered, and people from different nations greeted us. As I observed Ajmal interacting effortlessly with everyone, my admiration for him grew even more.

My mother-in-law entered with my sister-in-laws to greet us, and she hugged me warmly. "Molly," she said, "I am so glad that from now on, you are officially my daughter-in-law." While Ajmal attended to the guests, I bid goodbye to my father and friends. Interacting with numerous wedding attendees left me exhausted, so I stretched my legs on our bed and slowly took off my wedding dress, revealing a soft and lacy nightdress, likely the signature creation of a famous designer.

After changing, I needed to use the bathroom. Upon opening a side door in the room, I was astonished to find a walk-in closet that resembled a boutique, filled with the most expensive and fashionable clothes and accessories. While admiring myself in the mirror, Ajmal entered. Upon seeing what I was wearing, his expression changed, and he began speaking about the success of our marriage. Confused, I ran to the bathroom.

Upon returning, I found him still on the phone. "Don't stare, come sleep." After ten minutes, he joined me in bed, his arms circling around me. Shocked, I realized he was being affectionate. He smiled, kissed my forehead, and urged me to sleep. Exhausted, I succumbed to sleep in his arms.

Upon waking up, I attempted to disentangle myself from his embrace, but he pulled me closer, kissed me softly, and asked if I was awake. "Yeah," I replied. He inquired about my sleep, to which I responded, "Good, I guess." He teased me about sleeping in his arms, and we shared a tender moment. Ajmal then produced a beautiful red ruby ring surrounded by diamonds, promising to give me the world. Overwhelmed, I kissed him, and he declared me the sweetest person he had ever met.

As we prepared for breakfast, Ajmal inserted the ring on my right hand finger, expressing his warmth. "Let's have breakfast, dear, then we are ready to go!" he exclaimed. I agreed, and we hurried to catch a flight that was departing in 40 minutes.

In the car, Ajmal was busy with his phone, and I noticed that the speed was intentionally moderate, likely due to the desert surroundings. I began to appreciate the scenic views of marble mountains emerging from the stone and sand desert, with varying sand colors from silver-grey to rich red gold.

We landed at an airstrip in the jungle, and Molly was astonished to see the family's most expensive private jet. The interior of the jet resembled an apartment, with a master bedroom, en-suite bathroom, passenger seats, an office table, bar, kitchenette, and even a small library. Molly felt like she was in a lavish hotel.

Once settled in our seats, we were offered wine or juice before takeoff. Molly was living a dream. Giving up on sleep, Ajmal straightened in bed, and Molly, curled up next to him, maintained a connection with him even while sleeping.

When the air hostess brought refreshments, Molly opened her eyes, and Ajmal kissed her thoroughly. Molly glanced at her husband, who was in a romantic mood, looking hot in his casual attire. He playfully called her "Strawberry" and showered her with affection, even in front of the flight crew.

"Nah," she said while lowering her eyelashes, "Why are you looking at me like this?"

"What do you think it is, Mrs. Shallik?" he teased her again.

A blush colored her cheeks, and it was true what they say, that there's a thin line between love and hate, and in their case, it was only love.

He tugged her close, saying, "Ready for a world of our own? Come," his lips brushed her earlobes. "He could play me alive," she thought as he kissed her forehead. Together, they bid farewell to the flight crew and walked out of the aircraft, ready for a new chapter in their lives.

Outside, Molly silently observed the landscape. The breeze smelled of sand, and Ajmal inquired if she liked it. Molly was in awe and shared how coming here was a dream come true.

"Come, sweetheart," Ajmal said, "Come on, let's enjoy ourselves to the fullest. The waves of Maldives are waiting for you."

As they approached a lavish Bentley parked in front of them, Molly was astonished. This was an incredible car, a royal two-seater with a powerful engine. "Here we are, just you and me," he smiled, taking the keys from the guards.

"The security is intact, don't worry, but everybody will be invisible to us," he assured her.

The Maldives, with its sandy beaches, turquoise waters, and unique underwater marine life, was a tropical paradise. Molly had gathered this information before coming.

They were heading towards Fihalhohi Island, one of the most attractive places in the Maldives. Surrounded by shady coconut palm trees and clear waters, it was truly breathtaking. Ajmal explained that they would have a surreal experience with stunning views, excellent food, and a breathtaking island, adding with a mischievous smile that they would also have a private spa that was out of this world.

They played like teenagers on the shore, enjoying the beauty and connection between them. Ajmal gifted her a beautiful diamond and emerald pendant, and she blushed when he playfully mentioned wanting her to wear it during intimate moments.

Two years later, Molly walked into the garden and observed her family. Ajmal was sitting with their baby boy, Abbas, on his lap, and Noor was chatting away with her popsyy. Abbas had been born a year after their marriage, and he was just like his father.

Molly, who was expecting another child, sat down beside Ajmal. He noticed her change in demeanor and asked if she was okay. She revealed her pregnancy, and the happiness in Ajmal's eyes was unmistakable.

They celebrated the joyous news together, and Molly's heart swelled with love for her husband and their growing family. Their happy married life was something they had fought for and finally achieved.

And thus, they lived their happily ever after.

The story is a work of fiction. Any resemblance to actual persons, living or dead, events, or locations is purely coincidental. Writing is a passion I want to explore, and I have many ideas and thoughts to share, particularly centered around love stories. All my books will have happy endings, as I strongly believe in them.

Chapter 12

Early Days Of Royalty.

Molly sat in the garden, surrounded by the laughter of her family. Ajmal, holding their baby boy Abbas, and Noor, always the chatterbox, created a lively scene. The warmth of the desert air enveloped her as she watched her little family, and her heart swelled with contentment.

Ajmal, sensing a change in Molly's mood, turned to her and asked, "Are you okay, my love?" She met his gaze, a soft smile playing on her lips. "Remember when you were pregnant with Abbas?" he continued, a mischievous glint in his eyes.

"Every second of it," Molly replied, suppressing a smile.

"Yea," he chuckled, "you could eat for three people, always so hungry and cute."

"Oh, you only remember that?" she teased, giving him a sly look.

"So..." he trailed off, his eyes gleaming with excitement.

Molly took his hand and gently placed it on her stomach. "I'm pregnant, Ajmal."

Silence.

"Ajmal?" she called, concern flickering in her eyes.

Suddenly, he erupted into joy, lifting her off her feet and twirling her around. "We're having a baby!" he shouted, the sound echoing through the garden.

Molly couldn't help but giggle, overwhelmed by the sheer happiness radiating from her husband. Finally, he gently placed her back on her feet. "I'm so happy," he grinned, his eyes full of adoration.

Unable to contain her own joy, Molly leaned in and planted a kiss on his lips. As they broke the kiss, Ajmal whispered, "Thank you for giving me all this in my life, sugar. For our children, your love, and for staying in my country and adapting to its culture. I love you."

"I love you too, Ajmal," Molly whispered back, her heart brimming with love and gratitude.

Months passed, and the anticipation for the arrival of their new family member grew. The family was busy preparing for the new addition, and Noor was over the moon at the thought of becoming a big sister.

One evening, as the golden hues of the setting sun painted the sky, Molly and Ajmal found a quiet moment in the garden. The air was filled with the sweet fragrance of blooming flowers, creating a serene atmosphere.

Ajmal, his hand resting on Molly's blossoming belly, spoke softly, "Our life has been a beautiful journey, hasn't it?"

Molly nodded, "It's been more than I could have ever asked for."

Ajmal's eyes sparkled with love as he leaned in and placed a gentle kiss on Molly's forehead. "You're my everything, Molly. I can't wait to hold our little one in my arms and create even more beautiful memories."

The day arrived when their second child, a daughter they named Aisha, was born. The joy and laughter echoed through the Sheikh residence as the family celebrated the arrival of the newest member. Noor, now a proud big sister, couldn't contain her excitement.

As the days turned into weeks, and weeks into months, the Sheikh family continued to thrive. The laughter of children filled the air, and the love between Molly and Ajmal only deepened with time. Their home was a haven of joy, warmth, and, most importantly, love.

One evening, Ajmal surprised Molly with a romantic dinner under the stars. The garden was adorned with fairy lights, casting a soft glow over their surroundings. A gentle breeze played with Molly's hair as she sat across from Ajmal, the flickering candles creating a magical ambiance.

"I wanted tonight to be special," Ajmal said, his eyes locked onto Molly's. "To celebrate our love, our family, and our happily ever after."

Molly smiled, feeling a rush of gratitude for the wonderful life they had built together. The evening unfolded with laughter, shared memories, and promises for the future. As the night deepened, so did the intimacy between them.

Ajmal stood and extended his hand. "Dance with me, my queen."

Molly, her eyes sparkling with affection, took his hand. They swayed under the starlit sky, lost in each other's eyes. The world seemed to disappear, leaving only the two of them in a dance of love.

As the night reached its peak, Ajmal whispered words of love that sent shivers down Molly's spine. The air became charged with the heat of their passion, and the stars above witnessed a love that burned brighter than ever.

Their lips met in a fiery kiss, sealing their love once again. Under the celestial canopy, surrounded by the whispers of the night, Molly and Ajmal embraced the culmination of their journey—a journey marked by love, resilience, and the unwavering commitment to each other.

The Sheikh family continued to live their happily ever after, their love story an eternal flame that illuminated their lives and the lives of those around them.

Days turned into a routine of shared responsibilities and moments of bliss. The Sheikh family became a harmonious melody, each member contributing to the symphony of love and laughter. Aisha, the little princess, grew amidst the warmth of her family's affection.

One summer evening, the family decided to take a trip to the desert, a place that held a special significance in Molly and Ajmal's journey. The golden sands stretched out before them, mirroring the endless possibilities of their life together.

As they set up a small picnic, Noor, now a teenager, recounted stories of her childhood, filling the air with laughter. Molly and Ajmal exchanged knowing glances, their hearts brimming with pride and love for the family they had built.

Under the vast desert sky, Molly and Ajmal stole a moment to wander hand in hand. The sun cast an amber glow over the dunes, and Molly looked into Ajmal's eyes, grateful for the love that had sustained them through every twist of fate.

"I love you more with each passing day," Ajmal whispered, his voice a gentle caress.

Molly smiled, "Our love has weathered storms and blossomed like the desert rose. It's timeless."

The love between them remained passionate and deep, like an unending wellspring. They shared dreams, whispered promises, and created a future filled with love and shared adventures.

Years rolled by, and the Sheikh family grew, witnessing new milestones and overcoming fresh challenges. Aisha, now a spirited young woman, pursued her dreams, and Noor ventured into her own journey of love and companionship.

Ajmal's eyes gleamed with pride as he watched his daughters navigate through life, strong and confident. Molly, his eternal partner, stood by his side, their love a beacon that illuminated the path for the next generation.

One evening, as the sun dipped below the horizon, painting the sky in hues of orange and pink, Molly and Ajmal found themselves on the terrace of their home. The quiet beauty of the moment mirrored the serenity that had settled into their lives.

"Look at what we've built, Molly," Ajmal said, his arm around her shoulders.

"It's a tapestry of love," she replied, leaning into his embrace.

Their gaze lingered on the city below, the bustling streets, and the lights that twinkled like stars. Ajmal's voice broke the stillness, "I want to create a legacy of love, something that extends beyond our years."

Molly turned to him, her eyes reflecting the depth of their shared journey. "Our legacy is love, Ajmal. It lives in the laughter of our children, the stories we've shared, and the moments that define us."

The desert breeze carried whispers of a love story that had withstood the sands of time. Molly and Ajmal continued to navigate the journey of life hand in hand, their love an unwavering constant.

As the years continued to unfold, the Sheikh family embraced every chapter of their story. The pages were filled with joy, challenges, and an enduring love that surpassed the boundaries of time. Together, they walked into the sunset of each day, grateful for the love that had shaped their happily ever after.

In the quiet of their room, beneath the canopy of a velvet desert night, Molly and Ajmal found themselves alone. The air was heavy with anticipation, as if the very universe held its breath, waiting for the culmination of their love story.

The soft glow of candlelight bathed the room in a warm, golden hue. Molly, her heart racing, stood before Ajmal, her eyes locked with his, her body adorned in delicate lace that left little to the imagination. The gentle caress of silk sheets against her skin heightened her senses.

Ajmal, his dark eyes smoldering, slowly approached her. His fingers found the delicate straps of her lingerie, and with a single, lingering touch, he traced the outline of her collarbone. Molly's breath caught, and she closed her eyes for a moment, lost in the sensation.

With a tenderness that belied the fiery passion within him, Ajmal undressed Molly, his eyes never leaving hers. Each layer revealed more of her beauty, her vulnerability, her soul. The room was filled with an electrifying tension, a magnetic force that drew them closer together.

Moments later, they were entwined on the bed, their bodies creating a tapestry of desire. Their kisses were filled with longing, and their whispers of love hung in the air like an intoxicating perfume. Hands roamed, and fingers traced the contours of desire, each touch igniting a fire that burned hotter and brighter.

As the night deepened, the room echoed with the music of their love. Molly and Ajmal became one, their souls merging in a dance that defied time and space. It was a celebration of their love, a culmination of their journey, and an affirmation of their bond.

In the sacred hours of the night, their love reached its zenith. Molly and Ajmal lay in each other's arms, their hearts beating as one. The room was bathed in a soft, moonlit glow, a testament to the love that had ignited their souls.

"Forever," Ajmal whispered, his voice a promise that hung in the air.

"Forever," Molly echoed, her fingers tracing the contours of his face.

And there, under the stars of the desert night, Molly and Ajmal surrendered to the depths of their love, finding an eternity in each other's arms.

In the aftermath of their bold decision to choose love over duty, the palace found itself at the epicenter of both admiration and criticism. Whispers echoed through the grand halls, nobles debating the implications of Ajmal's choice to prioritize his heart.

Molly, now accustomed to navigating the intricacies of court life, became a symbol of resilience and unwavering love. Her every step, every word, was scrutinized. As the days unfolded, the couple faced both support and opposition from different corners of the kingdom.

Ajmal, undeterred, stood beside Molly. His love for her was a shield against the judgments that sought to tarnish their story. In private moments, away from the prying eyes, he whispered promises of eternity. "No matter what they say, Molly, you are my queen, my love, and that is an unbreakable bond."

The tension within the palace walls, however, was not the only challenge the couple faced. A storm brewed on the horizon—a political unrest threatening the very foundation of their rule. As Ajmal grappled with matters of the state, Molly found herself entangled in a web of palace intrigues.

Among the whispers, a figure emerged from the shadows—a long-lost relative, a cousin with a claim to the throne. The past, like a haunting ghost, returned to test the strength of Molly and Ajmal's commitment. Loyalties were questioned, alliances tested, and the kingdom teetered on the edge of uncertainty.

Molly, with newfound strength, navigated the treacherous waters of court politics. She delved into the history of the kingdom, uncovering secrets that had long been buried. With a keen mind and a compassionate heart, she became a force to be reckoned with, a queen in her own right.

In the midst of the turmoil, Molly discovered a clandestine plot that threatened not only their love but the very fabric of the kingdom. The revelation left her torn between loyalty to Ajmal and a responsibility to the people. She stood at a crossroads, the weight of the kingdom's fate resting on her shoulders.

With wisdom beyond her years, Molly devised a plan to expose the traitors within. Her courage, paired with Ajmal's unwavering support, brought the conspirators to justice. The kingdom, once shrouded in uncertainty, found a renewed sense of stability under their reign.

As the political storms subsided, Molly and Ajmal stole moments of respite in the quiet corners of the palace. The challenges they faced only strengthened the bond between them. Their love, tested by fire, emerged unscathed, a testament to the enduring power of a love that defied the odds.

One evening, beneath the star-studded desert sky, Ajmal led Molly to a secluded terrace. The air was filled with the heady scent of jasmine, and the moon cast a silvery glow over the sands. In that intimate setting, Ajmal took Molly's hands in his.

"My love," he began, his eyes reflecting the constellations above, "we've faced trials that would break most. Yet, here we stand—stronger, united. The kingdom is at peace, and my heart is at ease knowing you are by my side."

Molly's eyes glistened with unshed tears. "Ajmal, we've weathered storms, and our love has only deepened. I wouldn't trade these trials for a simpler path. Our journey, with all its twists and turns, has brought us here."

He dropped to one knee, a glint of mischief in his eyes. "Molly, my queen, will you renew our vows under the desert stars? A promise to face whatever comes our way, together."

Overwhelmed with emotion, Molly nodded. "Yes, a thousand times, yes."

The moon bore witness to their renewed vows, the desert breeze carrying their whispered promises into the night.

As seasons changed and years passed, Molly and Ajmal continued to rule their kingdom with wisdom and compassion. The challenges of their early years only served to strengthen the bonds of their love.

One fateful day, as the sun dipped below the dunes, casting hues of orange and pink across the sky, Molly felt a familiar flutter within. The kingdom celebrated as the news of an heir to the throne echoed through the land.

Their family, once a trio, now expanded. The joy of new life mirrored the rebirth of their love amidst the challenges. Ajmal, a doting father, found new purpose in the laughter of their child, and Molly reveled in the completeness of their family.

In the twilight of their years, Molly and Ajmal stood hand in hand, watching the sunset over the desert. The love that had ignited beneath the same sky now burned as a timeless flame. They had faced challenges, navigated treacherous paths, and emerged victorious.

As the sun dipped below the horizon, Molly leaned into Ajmal's embrace. "Forever," she whispered.

"Forever," he replied, the echo of their enduring love carried away by the desert winds.

Amid the blissful reign of Molly and Ajmal, a shadow from the past cast a haunting silhouette.

Chapter 13

The Mysterious Letter.

A mysterious letter, sealed with an ancient insignia, arrived at the palace. Its contents held the key to a secret long buried—the revelation of Molly's true lineage.

As Molly unfolded the weathered parchment, the weight of her destiny pressed upon her. The letter spoke of a forgotten lineage, a bloodline entwined with the very sands upon which the palace stood. Whispers of an ancient prophecy echoed through the words—an oath that bound Molly to a destiny far grander than she could have imagined.

Ajmal, ever the pillar of support, stood by Molly's side as she grappled with the truths hidden within the letter. The revelation stirred the winds of change, setting in motion a series of events that would challenge the very core of their love.

The prophecy spoke of a trial, a pilgrimage through the heart of the desert to uncover the secrets of Molly's heritage. It was a journey fraught with peril and mystery, an odyssey that beckoned them into the depths of the unknown.

The palace buzzed with preparations for the impending journey. The kingdom, still basking in the glow of stability, watched with bated breath as their queen embarked on a quest that transcended the boundaries of time. Ajmal, torn between duty and love, vowed to accompany Molly on this enigmatic pilgrimage.

As the sun dipped below the horizon, casting long shadows across the golden dunes, Molly and Ajmal set forth into the heart of the desert. The moon, a silent witness to their journey, illuminated their path with silver beams.

Their caravan, adorned with rich tapestries and guarded by loyal companions, traversed the vast expanse of the desert. Each night brought with it tales of old, shared by nomads who had roamed these lands for generations. Whispers of a forgotten kingdom, buried beneath the shifting sands, fueled the flames of curiosity within Molly's heart.

Amidst the ancient ruins that dotted the desert, Molly discovered murals that told the story of a once-great civilization. The images depicted a queen with eyes mirroring her own, a crown of stars adorning her brow. The parallels were uncanny, and the weight of destiny pressed upon Molly's shoulders.

As they ventured deeper into the desert, the trials grew more arduous. Sandstorms raged, testing the resilience of their spirits. Yet, with each challenge, Molly and Ajmal found strength in their love—a love that had weathered storms of both the heart and the kingdom.

In the heart of an oasis, surrounded by the whispers of ancient spirits, Molly encountered a wise oracle. The oracle, her eyes veiled by time, spoke in riddles that danced on the edge of comprehension. She foretold a choice—one that would determine not only Molly's destiny but the fate of the kingdom she ruled.

The choice, like a fork in the winding desert paths, loomed before Molly. It was a choice between the familiar comforts of the palace and the uncharted territories of her true heritage. Ajmal, his love unwavering, stood beside her as she grappled with the weight of destiny.

As the climax of their journey approached, Molly stood at the precipice of revelation. The ruins of an ancient city, hidden beneath the dunes, held the key to unlocking the mysteries of her lineage. With each step, the echoes of the past grew louder, urging Molly to embrace the destiny that awaited her.

In the heart of the forgotten city, Molly discovered a chamber adorned with celestial symbols. The walls whispered secrets of a celestial queen, a guardian of the desert realms. It was a legacy entwined with the very fabric of the universe—a legacy Molly now bore.

Ajmal, his eyes reflecting both pride and love, watched as Molly embraced her true identity. The ancient crown, once worn by queens of old, found a new resting place upon Molly's brow. It was a coronation that echoed through time, marking the convergence of past and present.

As they emerged from the depths of the desert, Molly and Ajmal carried with them the wisdom of the ages. The kingdom, awaiting their return, saw in Molly a queen transformed—a sovereign not only of the people but also of the celestial realms.

The air in the palace changed upon their return. Whispers of the pilgrimage, the revelation of Molly's true lineage, spread through the kingdom. The people, ever loyal, celebrated the union of their beloved queen with the ancient legacy she now embodied.

In the quiet of their chamber, beneath the celestial canopy of the desert night, Molly and Ajmal reflected on the journey that had tested the boundaries of their love. The trials, the revelations, and the choices made in the heart of the desert had sculpted a new chapter in the annals of their love story.

As the moon cast its silver glow over the palace, Molly leaned into Ajmal's embrace. "We've walked a path few would dare to tread, my love," she whispered.

Ajmal, the moonlight reflecting in his eyes, replied, "And in that path, we found not only our destinies but the eternity of our love."

Their love, now intertwined with the celestial legacy, became a beacon that illuminated the kingdom. The palace, once a symbol of power, transformed into a sanctuary where the threads of destiny and love wove a tapestry that transcended time.

In the years that followed, Molly and Ajmal ruled with a wisdom that echoed the lessons learned beneath the desert stars. The kingdom flourished, and their love became a legend whispered in the winds that swept through the palace corridors.

One fateful night, as the desert winds carried the echoes of a thousand tales, Molly and Ajmal stood atop the palace terrace. The stars, like witnesses to the tapestry of their love, twinkled in silent approval.

Molly, her eyes reflecting the constellations above, turned to Ajmal. "Our love story, my king, is etched in the stars."

Ajmal, the moonlight kissing his features, replied, "And as long as the stars illuminate the desert sky, our love will endure."

In that moment, beneath the celestial expanse, Molly and Ajmal sealed their love with a promise—an eternal vow that echoed through the sands of time.

End Note from the Author:

Dear readers, as we bid farewell to Molly and Ajmal, may their love story linger in your hearts. Love, with all its complexities and triumphs, is a journey worth embracing. May your own tales of love be as timeless as the desert winds.

Author's Note

As I pen down the pages of "The Royal Love," I want to express my deepest gratitude to the pillars of my life, my unwavering support system – my family.

To my son, Prabhjot Anand, and his wife, Molika Anand, who have been my strength and endless inspiration, and to my cutest grandson, Vyohh Anand, a bundle of joy at just eight months old, you bring boundless happiness to my life.

My daughter, Ekleen Sethi, and my son-in-law, Gagandeep Sethi, along with my two precious grandchildren, Tiana and Rida, have always filled my life with laughter and warmth. Your love is a treasure I hold dear.

To my friends, my confidants and critics, your encouragement and feedback have been invaluable. This journey wouldn't be the same without you.

My brother, Harvinder Singh Bakshi, and sister, Harmeet Kaur Dham, whose unwavering belief in me has fueled my creative spirit, and my late mother, whose memory continues to guide me – you all reside in my heart and soul, and your presence is palpable in every word I write.

And to my husband, who stood by me through thick and thin, even though life had other plans for us – you remain the love story that inspires all my tales.

It's with immense love and gratitude that I dedicate this work to each of you. Your love, support, and presence in my life have made "The Royal Love" possible.

With love,
Sukhwant Kaur Anand(Lily)

www.ingramcontent.com/pod-product-compliance
Lightning Source LLC
LaVergne TN
LVHW061559070526
838199LV00077B/7117